BACKYARD WITCH

Sadie's Story

by Christine Heppermann and Ron Koertge

illustrated by Deborah Marcero

Greenwillow Books, *An Imprint of* HarperCollins *Publishers*

Backyard Witch: Sadie's Story
Text copyright © 2015 by Christine Heppermann and Ron Koertge;
illustrations copyright © 2015 by Deborah Marcero

All rights reserved. No part of this book may be used or reproduced in any manner whatsoever without written permission except in the case of brief quotations embodied in critical articles and reviews. Printed in the United States of America. For information address HarperCollins Children's Books, a division of HarperCollins Publishers, 195 Broadway, New York, NY 10007.
www.harpercollinschildrens.com
The text of this book is set in Berling Roman.
Book design by Sylvie Le Floc'h

Library of Congress Cataloging-in-Publication Data
Heppermann, Christine, author.
Sadie's story / by Christine Heppermann and Ron Koertge ; pictures by Deborah Marcero.
    pages cm.—(Backyard witch)
    "Greenwillow Books."
Summary: When her two best friends take a vacation without her, nine-year-old Sadie meets a witch who takes her on a bird-watching adventure. Includes birding tips.
    ISBN 978-0-06-233838-9 (trade ed.)
[1. Friendship—Fiction. 2. Witches—Fiction. 3. Bird watching—Fiction.] I. Koertge, Ronald, author. II. Marcero, Deborah, illustrator. III. Title.
    PZ7.1.H47Sad 2015 [Fic]—dc23 2014029443

15 16 17 18 19 CG/RRDH 10 9 8 7 6 5 4 3 2 1
First Edition

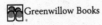 Greenwillow Books

*For Audrey, who gives me
inspiration and only charges
fifty cents—C. H.*

*For Bianca and Jan, who
work for free—R. K.*

*For Esther, my very own
Ms. M—D. M.*

Contents

Chapter 1
Poof

Sadie didn't want to hear one more word about Moose Butt Lake.

Really it was Moose Head Lake, but Jess said "Moose Head Lake Moose Head Lake Moose Head Lake" so many times that Sadie couldn't stand it.

Moose Butt Lake, where Jess and Maya

would make s'mores after dinner or maybe walk to the little store near Jess's grandparents' cabin for super-special Moose Butt ice cream.

Moose Butt Lake, where Jess and Maya would lie on the dock at sunset and watch the bats come out of Moose Butt Cave.

"You know," said Sadie, "bats have rabies."

"Not at Moose Head Lake," Jess assured her.

Of course, thought Sadie. Special Moose Butt Lake bats.

Moose Butt Lake, where there were two kayaks, one for Jess and one for Maya. They didn't need a third for Sadie because Sadie wasn't coming.

"This is the first year they've let me bring a friend to Moose Head Lake," Jess reminded her for the billionth time that morning as the three girls huddled in the window seat in Sadie's den. "Maybe next summer I can bring you, too."

Maya stopped scratching Sadie's cat, Wilson, under the chin and patted Sadie's knee. "We'll only be gone four days, which in geologic time is like a nanosecond. Like a fraction of a nanosecond. We're practically already back!"

3

"Trust me, you won't want to come back," Jess said. "When I was five, I hid in the boathouse when it was time to go home. BeMaw and BePaw had to drag me out of there kicking and screaming."

Sadie felt like kicking and screaming at that very moment. But, of course, she didn't.

"What Jess intended but neglected to say," said Maya, "is that we won't have nearly as much fun without you."

"Well, duh, Ms. Dictionary," said Jess. "But, Sadie, I swear I begged them—"

Sadie cut Jess off mid-excuse. "Don't worry about it. I'll be okay."

"I know you will." Jess reached for Sadie's ponytail, divided it into three sections, and started to braid.

"At least I won't get rabies," Sadie mumbled.

"What?" asked Jess, tugging the hair perhaps a little harder than absolutely necessary.

"I said, just don't forget to write me. A postcard or something."

"And one for Wilson, too," Maya promised.

"Hey, down there!" Sadie's mother's voice boomed from the top of the stairs. "I just talked to Jess's mom. Time for you girls to get a move on."

Which is how Sadie found herself standing at the front door watching her two best friends, arms slung around each other's shoulders, start down the sidewalk. She waved. Maya waved back. Jess blew theatrical kisses. Then they rounded the corner onto Oxley Street and disappeared.

Poof.

Sadie contemplated the rest of the day. And the day after that. And after that. All the lonely hours ahead closing around her like a collapsed tent.

She drifted back to the window seat and curled next to Wilson, who was watching a single brown bird peck at the dirt. "Good thing one of us is easily entertained," she said, petting him.

She tried to read, but it wasn't easy, what with Jess and Maya probably already in the minivan, speeding toward adventure. Though, really, what was so special about their plans? Burned marshmallows? Nasty flying rodents pooping in their hair? Not that she wanted that to happen, but . . .

Beside her, Wilson startled. He jumped to his feet, skittered across her lap, and pawed at the glass.

"What?" Sadie said, setting down *More Tales from Grimm*. "It's only the backyard." Only the grass her mother mowed, only the flowers her father watered. Only the green patio chairs. Only her old playhouse over by the garage.

Wilson's tail twitched. He mewed.

"Okay, I'll let you out. But don't bring home anything gross."

Sadie lifted the window.

Zip! Wilson was gone. He streaked across the flagstones, past the petunias and Queen Anne's lace, right to the playhouse. Well, not *to*, exactly. He stopped a few yards away and froze except for his tail, which swished back and forth like a windshield wiper.

Why was he acting like that?

Then she saw it. An almost invisible wisp of smoke rising from the playhouse roof.

Maybe she had imagined it. She blinked.

The smoke was still there.

Chapter 2
Britches for Witches

In the kitchen she found her father, fussing with his blender. Sliced fruit lay everywhere. "This is going to be the best smoothie ever," he announced without turning around.

"Dad, I think the playhouse is on fire!"

"What, sweetheart?"

"Look!"

Clutching a kiwi, her father followed her over to the window. Squinted. Took off his eyeglasses, cleaned them with his shirtsleeve, and put them back on. "No smoke, no flames. Everything looks okay to me."

Sadie stared hard at the patch of sky above the playhouse. There was no trace of white, not even a cloud. The smoke was gone. If it had ever been there in the first place.

"Besides, the playhouse is plastic. If it was burning, we'd smell dioxin. All I smell is"—he stuck his nose down by the open windowsill—"a neighbor cooking something yummy."

"I guess," she said. "But I think I'll double-check."

Her father chuckled and kissed the top of

her head. "Let me know if we need to call the fire brigade." He returned to the counter, dropped the kiwi, and scooped up some mango. He popped a piece into his mouth. "Heaven!" he exclaimed between chews. "Want to try a bite of heaven, Sadie?"

"Sure. When I get back."

Outside she filled the watering can with the hose. Just in case.

Through the gap between two blue plastic shutters she spied a flash of black. Something was moving! Or someone. And what was that strange smell? Like the something-someone

was baking a cake out of orange peels, cinnamon, and . . . bicycle tires?

One step. Two steps. Before she knew it she stood at the playhouse door. The door she'd opened a thousand times before while playing with Jess and Maya. But this time she had no idea what she'd find on the other side.

She crouched, setting down the watering can. She raised her fist to knock. She lowered her fist. She raised it again.

Jess wouldn't be scared. Jess would have burst through the door already without knocking at all.

Rap, rap. "Hello?" Sadie called softly. Then with more volume, "Hello?"

Silence. Wilson pressed his whole body

against her calves as if trying to nudge her forward.

She knocked again. "I know someone is in there."

"I'm not hurting anything," said a thin, scratchy voice.

"That's good. But what are you doing?"

"Just a minor hex."

"A minor hex? Something's on fire!"

"Not really." The voice was stronger now. "Everything's under control."

Hunched in the dirt with one hand on the pink plastic doorknob, Sadie paused to, as Maya would say, evaluate. There had to be a logical explanation. "Are you homeless?" she asked.

"Not anymore."

"Running away?"

"I'm a little old for that."

"So you're a grown-up."

"Dearie me, no. Not one of those dull, horrid specimens."

Not sure what to do next, Sadie glanced down at Wilson. He stared at her mutely. She tried again. "Okay. But who are you?"

"Why don't you and Wilson come inside and see?"

Sadie slowly opened the door. There, beside a bubbling cauldron, stood a tiny woman holding a long wooden spoon. She was dressed all in black—black smock dress, black pointy shoes, black pointy hat.

Sadie began, "You're not a—"

"I am."

"Anybody can put on a costume."

"True. But their 'costumes,' as you put it, don't come from Britches for Witches."

The tiny woman took off her hat, revealing matted gray hair. She flipped the hat over. "Read the label."

Sadie peered inside the sturdy felt cone. "It does say 'Britches for Witches.'"

"Surely you've heard their jingle." The woman cleared her throat noisily and sang, "Britches for Witches. Black cats and hats. Broomsticks and cauldrons and thousands of gnats."

"Gnats?"

"For annoyance spells. Very useful at picnics."

Sadie couldn't stand all the way up in the little doorway, so she duck-walked a few steps forward. "If you're a real witch, prove it."

"How about this: did you see me sneak into your playhouse?"

"No."

"Exactly. I just appeared. Poof!"

Wilson sniffed at the cauldron, the contents of which glopped and gurgled until the woman gave them a brisk stir.

"But I haven't been staring at my playhouse all day," Sadie countered. "Could you do something more . . . supernatural?"

"Like a trick?"

"Yes."

"A trick is by definition meant to deceive. I don't want to deceive you. Why don't you sit down, Sadie, and let's get to know each other?"

"How did you know my name? I didn't tell you my name. Come to think of it, I didn't tell you Wilson's name, either."

The woman's smile was a bit snaggle-toothed, but it seemed friendly. "Sit down, my dear."

Sadie sat.

Chapter 3

Just Doing Magic
with a Friend

Somehow, even with all three of them, plus the cauldron, the space inside the playhouse did not feel cramped.

Wilson, normally wary of strangers, settled down at the witch's feet and closed his eyes. Not quite proof that the woman was magical, Sadie decided, but pretty solid

evidence that she was, well, different.

Raising the spoon to her lips, the witch sipped and cocked her head. "It needs something," she said finally.

"What are you making? Is it a potion?" Sadie imagined Jess and Maya calling from the road and asking what she was up to. *Oh, nothing much. Just doing magic with a friend. Nobody you know.*

"It's soup," the witch said.

"For the hex?"

"For lunch. I finished the hex. Next I have to work on a spell. After that, a nap. I wonder if you could find me a blanket."

"Now?"

"Please."

Sadie crawled back out into the bright

afternoon sun. "C'mon, Wilson," she called over her shoulder. The cat blinked but otherwise didn't move. Great. Even Wilson was deserting her. A couple more defections and she'd be an orphan.

"May I keep him here?" asked the witch. "Just for a little while."

"Aren't you supposed to have a cat of your own?" Sadie said grumpily.

The witch shook her head. "Long story. After the blanket, perhaps."

On the way to her room, Sadie passed her mother upside-down against a wall in the hallway.

"How about coming along to the studio with me later?" Her mother worked as a yoga instructor. Sadie was accustomed to having conversations with her mother's feet.

"No, thanks."

"Are you sure? I don't want you wandering in and out of the study every few minutes. Dad took the summer off from teaching to write his book, not to listen to you moan about how bored you are."

Looking directly at her mother's ankles, Sadie answered, "I'm not bored. Not anymore."

"Well, good for you, honey. Keep your spirits up. Your friends will be home soon. If you start to miss them, take deep cleansing breaths."

"Okay." Sometimes Sadie wondered if spending all that time on her head had dented her mother's brain.

A quick rummage through the bin at the foot of her bed produced what the witch had requested. She tucked the blanket under her arm, not hiding it exactly, just trying to avoid pestering questions from her father, who stopped her at the back door with two glasses of foamy purple liquid.

"Here," he said, handing her a glass. "This will make us feel young."

"Dad, I am young. I'm nine. Besides, you're supposed to be writing."

"That's what the blueberries are for. To recharge my creative energy. Though maybe I should have added kale. . . ." He shuffled off in the direction of the kitchen, mumbling something about antioxidants.

Sadie took the smoothie back to the playhouse, where she gave the witch her

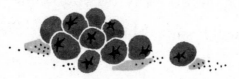

old,   light   pink blanket with the chubby yellow ducklings all over it. Her baby blanket. A babyish blanket, she realized, noting the one shriveled corner she used to suck on when she was little. How embarrassing.

But the witch stroked the soft fabric and murmured, "This is perfect, Sadie. Thank you." She folded the blanket and tucked it away in the corner. Then she said, "The soup should simmer for a while. How about we tackle that spell?"

We. Sadie almost dropped her smoothie. "You want me to help?"

"Of course. Why do you think I came?" The witch smiled broadly at her. "Now let's head outside. This particular enchantment requires a bit more room."

Facing each other in the yard, the witch and Sadie measured almost the same height, though the witch's pointy hat made her seem taller. Music from the classical radio station Sadie's father always listened to trickled from the open kitchen window. "Could we move behind the playhouse?" Sadie asked. "I don't want my parents to see us."

"What would they see? Just two friends casting an innocent spell."

"It's that part about the spell that worries me."

"I'm sure they wouldn't mind you helping a sorceress in need, but whatever makes you more comfortable, dear."

A squirrel scrabbling across the back fence stopped briefly to gawk at them, spied Wilson, and kept going. The witch positioned Sadie near the lilacs and took four big steps to stand across from her. "I'll begin the incantation, and you follow along."

"Is this dangerous?" Sadie was almost breathless.

"Not at all," the witch assured her. "It's a simple finder spell, but if done right, it can be very powerful." She closed her eyes and began chanting softly.

"Excuse me, should I be doing something?" Sadie interrupted.

The witch opened her eyes. "That was just the preliminaries. We're ready now."

Sadie's whole body tingled, the way it did

when she rode a roller coaster up a steep hill or looked down from the edge of the high diving board or had to stand up in front of the class to recite a poem. *Here we go.*

Solemnly, the witch crooned, "Put your right leg in." She extended a pointy-toed shoe in front of her like a ballet dancer. Sadie copied the motion. "Put your right leg out." She stretched her leg behind her, and Sadie did the same. "Put your right leg in. And, summoning all the turbulence in all the spheres of heaven, shake it all about."

Instead of mimicking the witch's wild flailing, Sadie just stood there. "This isn't a spell. It's the hokey-pokey!"

"I beg your pardon. In my circles, we call it the hocus-pocus."

"How can it be magical?" Sadie said as she watched the witch slow to a wibble, then a wobble, then a quiver. "I did the hokey-pokey last month at my uncle's wedding."

"And you found things, didn't you?" said the witch, struggling to catch her breath. "The church? The reception hall? The cake?"

"Yes, but . . ."

"Okay, then. Now let's turn ourselves around." She revolved slowly in a circle.

After a moment's hesitation, Sadie revolved, too, and then, once they were face-to-face again, said, "I don't think this is working."

As if Sadie's words were scissors cutting the strings that held the witch up, she sagged. Drooped. Sank to the ground in a puddle of black dress. "I'm not sure of anything anymore. I am an optimist by nature, but I am starting to wonder if I will ever find them."

Sadie sat beside her in the grass. "What are you looking for?"

"Not what. Whom. Two whoms. Ethel and Onyx." Wilson padded over, waded across the witch's skirt, and climbed into her lap.

She scratched him forcefully behind the ears before saying, "The soup should be ready now. We'll have lunch, and I'll tell you a story."

"I'd like that," Sadie said, hoping she sounded encouraging. "I like stories." For the first time she noticed the witch's eyes. Beneath the crinkled lids they were green, the same as her own.

"I do, too, dear. I just wish this one had a happier ending."

Chapter 4
No More Llama Drool

"Soup?" The witch held out a teacup from Sadie's old, blue toy tea set.

"No, thanks." Sadie jiggled the smoothie. "This is pretty filling. Dad made it."

They were back inside the playhouse, door shut, seated at the little plastic table. Wilson, showing no interest in smoothies or soup, settled on the baby blanket and began the nap portion of the afternoon.

"Is your father in the potion business, too?"

Sadie laughed. "It's just fruit and yogurt."

"Ah, that takes me back to Potions 101. We started with fruit and yogurt."

The witch blew on the contents of her teacup to cool it and took a tentative sip. "I know what's missing!" From somewhere near her feet she produced a worn black bag. She dug around inside it until she pulled out a small glass jar labeled "Oregano." But when she shook the jar over her cup, only a few dusty green flakes fell out. "Well, that's a pity," she said, returning the jar to the bag. "I used to just pop over to Ethel's for more. We were always running back and forth to each

other's cottages to borrow things. A pinch of oregano here. A cup of llama drool there."

"So your neighbor had llama drool?" Sadie asked as she wiped her purple mustache on her arm.

The witch nodded. "Neighbor and best friend. Ethel lived right next door to me."

"In the forest," Sadie added.

"In Milwaukee."

"In a gingerbread cottage?"

"Hardly." The witch shivered. "Milwaukee gets cold in the winter. Anyway, Ethel had a nice home and a job she loved."

"Don't all witches love their jobs?" said Sadie. "I would." She wouldn't mind, say, having the power to make the water in a certain moose-themed lake disappear.

"Being a witch isn't a job, it's a calling. Ethel was a pastry chef."

"Was?"

"A sad verb, don't you agree?" A fat black ant crawled across the table onto the witch's hand and into the folds of her sleeve, reappearing at her collar. With her finger she made an elevator to gently lower the ant back onto the ground.

"I'm sorry," Sadie murmured, staring down into her smoothie.

"Oh no, sweetheart, Ethel didn't die. Not as far as I know. But she did leave. Left her cottage. Left her job at Cake Charmer. Left me."

"Where did she go?"

"Well, it was fall, so I expect she flew south with all the others."

"And there wasn't enough room for you, so you weren't invited," Sadie said, her face growing hot with indignation. "I know how that goes."

"No, no." The witch flapped her small arms. "She flew. She turned into a bird. A yellow warbler. And not by choice, I'm fairly certain."

Sadie's heart did a little flip of excitement. Now they were getting somewhere. She leaned forward. "So Ethel was cursed?"

"Careless is more like it. I told her a thousand times, 'Wear your glasses when you bake or hex!' But oh no, Ethel knew best. So it was adder's eyelid instead of almond extract. Cactus instead of cardamom. With a recipe, that means customers spitting out their scones. With a spell, it means she's five inches tall and *chip-chip-chip*-ing her head off. That's how I found her. And that's when I saw Onyx, my cat, stalking her."

Horrified, Sadie looked over at Wilson and pictured tiny, feathered versions of Jess and Maya dangling from his jaws. "What did you do?"

"Well, there was no time for my Whoops-I-Didn't-Mean-to-Do-That Anti-Hex potion,

even if I'd had the gargoyle scales, which I seriously doubt. So I grabbed Onyx and tossed him out. But when I opened the front door, out flew Ethel, too. So there I was, without my two best friends. I haven't seen either of them since."

"They'll come back," Sadie said.

"One can only hope." The witch sighed and leaned over the cauldron, out of which, curiously enough, soap bubbles now floated. "Shall I wash and you dry?"

As Sadie swirled a black dishtowel around inside the clean teacup, she said, "My two best friends left this morning."

"And you miss them."

Sadie hesitated. "Sort of. I guess. I mean, yes."

The witch raised her eyes from the suds. "Which is it?"

"It's just that Jess can be so . . . Jess-like."

The witch peeled dishwashing gloves from her gnarled hands. She tossed them into the black bag and said, "At least your Jess knows which way she's going. Birds get blown off course. Take a wrong turn at the third cloud from the left. Who can predict where a bird will end up? Especially a stubborn yellow warbler who takes off half-blind without her spectacles. It's all so frustrating!"

Sparks shot from the witch's fingertips.

With a screech, Wilson leaped straight into the air.

The playhouse filled with thick gray smoke.

Chapter 5
Big Black Bag

"Wow," said Sadie after her coughing subsided.

The witch flicked the baby blanket at the last of the smoke to shoo it out the window. "Cozy and better than mugwort for protection!" she croaked, beaming at the ducky-covered cloth.

Sadie looked over at Wilson, who was in the corner washing his front paw, trying to recover his dignity. "I guess Onyx left because his feelings were hurt," she said. Wilson bobbed his head in what was either a nod of agreement or a vigorous attempt to lick the fur on his chest.

"There's really no excuse for how I behaved," said the witch. "Shouting at him. Banning him from the cottage." A small puff of gray smoke that must have been hiding near the ceiling floated down and hovered over the witch's head like a thundercloud. She waved her arms in the air to disperse it. Then she said, "I know he can take care of himself, but I wish he'd come back and let me apologize."

"I bet he will," Sadie said. "Jess and Maya and I fight sometimes, but then we make up. Friends don't stay mad forever." As if to prove her point, Wilson padded over and butted his head against the witch's fingers, asking to be petted. A peace offering.

"I do sometimes worry in the middle of the night." The witch gathered Wilson into her lap. "What if Onyx is cold or hurt? What if Ethel is somewhere with a lot of cats? Like the Catskills."

"Aren't those just mountains?"

"Nevertheless."

"Once Wilson was missing for two days. I thought he was gone forever, but he was just locked in a neighbor's garage.

He was fine. Except for

knocking over the potting soil. He thought it was kitty litter."

Stroking Wilson's back all the way down to the tip of his tail, the witch said, "You're right, dear, I should think positively." But she sounded so droopy and sad that Sadie couldn't stand it for one single second longer. "You know what? We should find Ethel and Onyx."

"Well, as I told you, I've tried." Suddenly the witch's face brightened. "But I do have a new idea. Just being around someone like you gives me so much energy!"

Gently she scooted Wilson out of the way, reached into her black bag, and began taking out things. Little pouches of things. Little vials of things. Little boxes of things. Little pinches of things.

Sadie watched with growing delight. "Are all those magical?"

"What in the world isn't magical? Nobody understands electricity. Not really. And look at penicillin. It grows on bread! You think that isn't magical?" She shook one of the baggies. "These are herbs, mostly. Borage for courage. Wolfsbane for invisibility."

"I've always wanted to be invisible," said Sadie. Although, she had to admit, sometimes she felt invisible already. Like she could stomp her feet, hold her breath until she turned magenta, and no one would notice. Okay, Maya might notice. Might say a few comforting big words. Still, that wouldn't stop her from linking arms with Jess and going away.

"Being invisible would help," the witch mused. "We wouldn't frighten Ethel when she landed. She doesn't know you, and she's shy. The thing is, I can never find the wolfsbane."

The witch reached deeper into the bag. "But it works. I think. I have an acquaintance named Zelda who's always saying how invisible she is, but it's inevitably after the fact. She's all, 'Oh, I was so invisible yesterday.' Or, 'You should have not seen me last week.' Here it is!"

"You found the wolfsbane?"

"No, but I found what I was looking for," the witch said, her arm still buried.

"Oh, good! Is it a book of spells handed down from forever?"

"Not exactly."

"Is it a wand made from an enchanted tree?"

"No."

"But it will help us find Ethel and maybe Onyx?"

"Oh yes. Close your eyes and hold out your hands."

Her palms prickling with anticipation, Sadie did as she was told.

Chapter 6
The Park

"Really?" Sadie stared at the binoculars in her grip. "No spells or potions? No eye of newt or tongue of toad?"

The witch waved her hand dismissively. "Been there, done that. And between you and me, eye of gecko is cheaper and just as effective."

She lifted a second pair of binoculars, pointed them out the window, and adjusted the focus. "I've been a bird-watcher all my life, and I can tell you, the most powerful magic is something anyone can do. It's called paying attention."

"But why look for Ethel here?"

"Well, since she's a ditz about directions, she could have ended up anywhere. Here seems like as good a place as any. Shall we go for a walk and see what we can see?"

"Both of us?" Sadie asked, eyebrows

raised. "Out in the neighborhood? Um, together?"

"Of course. There's a lovely park nearby. I'm sure you know it. We could start there."

"I'll be right back," Sadie said finally.

She found her father in the study, yelling at his laptop. "Helvetica Bold! Who told you to change the font to Helvetica Bold?"

She tiptoed through the maze of books and papers scattered across the floor and stood directly behind him. "Dad, I'm going to the playground for a while."

"Fine, fine. Have fun. And take Helvetica Bold with you!" he said, still scowling at the screen.

"Actually, I'm going with a witch. From Milwaukee."

"Is she? That's nice, sweet pea. Grab a sweatshirt before you go."

Sadie would grab a sweatshirt, but not for warmth and not for herself, either.

A few minutes later she presented the witch with a purple hoodie and a pair of old jeans that she'd rescued from the giveaway bag.

"A disguise," Sadie explained. "Because if you're all in black with a pointy hat, everyone will look at us looking for Ethel."

The witch examined the hoodie critically. "I wish this said 'I Love Bowling' instead of 'I Love Gymnastics.' Ethel and I used to bowl in a league every Thursday night against the Mid-City Shamans."

"I'm trying to picture that," said Sadie.

She turned her head away politely while the witch changed.

Then off they went.

Past the Goldbarths', where Binky, a dachshund with the personality of a tiger

shark, lunged at their ankles through the chain-link fence.

Past the Simonsons', whose sprinkler watered the grass, the sidewalk, and half the street.

"I'm melting!" shrieked the witch as they dashed under the spray.

"What . . ."

"Just a joke."

Past Jess's house, where the drawn curtains, garage doors shut tight, and general no-one-is-home-ness started Sadie feeling sorry for herself all over again. The witch grabbed her hand and pulled her along.

"Now, this is nice," said the witch when they reached the entrance to the park.

And it was. Picnic tables, giant oak trees,

a tire swing, a twisty slide that was the closest Sadie ever came to flying, except on hot days when her thighs stuck to the molded metal.

"Let's sit over there." The witch headed for a table in the shade.

"I don't see any birds," said Sadie once they were settled.

"You will."

The witch lay back on the top of the picnic table, and beside her, Sadie did the same. Yet no matter which way Sadie swiveled her binoculars, they showed her nothing but leaves and branches and empty blue sky.

Well, she couldn't blame the birds for staying away with all the noise in the playground. Toddlers squealing. Mothers chattering and laughing. A little girl wailing from the top of the jungle gym while her dad, arms raised, hollered "Jump!" A swing creaking as it arced back and forth.

Wait, was that really a swing? She sat up.

Screek!

Sadie practically fell off the picnic table.

The witch jutted out her chin, flattened her lips, and made the sound again, louder.

And from somewhere close by came an answer: *Screek! Screek!*

Chapter 7
Call Me Ms. M

"Blue jay," the witch confirmed. "That's his squeaky gate call. They also have calls that sound like bells."

She pursed her lips and made a high-pitched *pip*. "I had a pair nesting outside my kitchen window. Kept thinking my cauldron timer was going off."

Pip. Pip. All of a sudden the blue jay was there, winging its way through the trees to perch near the drinking fountain.

"Oh, look, dear, isn't he gorgeous?" said the witch in a hushed voice.

At that moment Sadie *did* have a magical power, though she didn't know what to call it. All she knew was that the park had transformed. Or she had. Or now the park trusted her enough to share its secrets.

A bush she'd thought was simply rustling in the breeze became alive with small brown sparrows.

"Song sparrows, I believe," said the witch. "See the dark splotch on that one's chest? Like he has a leaky pen in his shirt pocket."

What at first had looked like pinecones

scattered across the dirt turned into black-capped chickadees pecking for seed. "I do so admire a creature who shares my affinity for hats," said the witch.

A dancing yellow leaf grew wings before Sadie's eyes and sailed up to land on the basketball hoop. She tapped the witch's shoulder excitedly and pointed.

"Hmmm. The coloration isn't quite vibrant enough for a warbler. I think that's an oriole. If only I could find my field guide. Drat that wolfsbane. It spilled in my bag and got all over everything."

They watched and listened for at least an hour. A robin tugged a fat worm from the grass and scurried away with it to dine in private. Three crows bickered by the sandbox. A male and female cardinal played tag from branch to branch. It was all so interesting that Sadie almost forgot about Ethel.

"Tomorrow," said the witch. "I have a good feeling about tomorrow."

On the way home, Sadie worked up the courage to ask the witch something she'd been thinking about, but before she could open her mouth, the witch said, "You learned the names of all of these different birds, and now you want to know my name."

"It does seem a little strange for me to just call you 'witch.'"

"No stranger than my real name." The witch stopped to shake a pebble out of her pointy shoe. "My mother meant well, but . . ."

Mr. Tucker from up the street drove by and waved. Did he turn around to gawk once he reached the intersection, or was Sadie just being a worrywart?

"My first name is—are you ready for this?—Morgan."

"That's not bad at all!"

"Morgan Le Fay was a famous sorceress. But Morgan rhymes with Gorgon." She looked at Sadie and waited. "The monsters from Greek mythology with snakes for hair?"

"Oh," said Sadie.

"Exactly. Morgan the Gorgon. Grade school was a total nightmare."

"My middle name is Lotus," Sadie confessed. "After a yoga position. And a flower. Eric Myers found out and said it sounded like 'blowfish.' That's what the boys called me all first grade."

They strolled in silence, shoulders almost touching, until the witch said, "Sadie is a lovely name. It suits you. And you can call me what Ethel calls me. What she used to call me when she could talk." The witch smiled her crooked smile. "Ethel called me Ms. M. I rather like it."

Sadie smiled back wider than she'd smiled in days, maybe wider than she'd smiled all year. "Yes," she said. "I like it too, Ms. M."

Chapter 8
Sweet Dreams

In the backyard they parted ways, Ms. M into the playhouse, Wilson trotting at her heels, and Sadie into the kitchen for dinner.

"There you are." Her mother, in purple tights and a yellow tank top, stood balanced on one leg in front of the stove. The sole of her opposite foot rested against her thigh. Sadie knew the name of that yoga pose: tree pose. Imagining the birds from the park perched on her mother's "branches," she giggled.

"You're all bright-eyed and bushy-tailed," remarked her father as he entered from the study. "I knew that smoothie would perk you right up. Should we set the table?" He opened the silverware drawer.

"It's so nice out," said her mother, transferring the contents of the wok onto a big platter. "Why don't we eat on the patio?"

"NO!"

Both her parents stared at her. Mom held up a wooden spoon like a torch, Dad a fistful of forks.

"I mean," Sadie said, trying to steady her voice, "there are thousands of mosquitoes out

there." She scratched three or four places.

"Thousands," her mother said. "That sounds crowded. We'll eat in here. Let me just check the rice."

Her father set the steaming platter in the center of the table, leaned over it, and sniffed. "Mmmm, ginger. I feel my sinuses clearing already."

Sadie stared at the mound of limp vegetables, most of which were the same shade of drab green. Probably right now Jess's grandfather was flipping juicy hamburgers at the grill. But at least she'd succeeded in keeping her parents out of the backyard. What if they'd heard a suspicious cackle? Smelled leftover soup?

Facts were facts: She had a witch in her

playhouse. A nice witch. An interesting witch. But a witch nonetheless. If her parents discovered Ms. M, they'd never let her stay. Not in a million years. Then there'd be no Jess, no Maya, and no Ms. M. Sadie would be alone. Again.

For a while they ate in silence, her mother methodically chewing and, Sadie knew, silently counting to thirty-two, the key to perfect digestion.

"I haven't seen Wilson all afternoon," her father said finally. "I hope he's not locked in Virginia's garage again."

"HE'S ASLEEP!" More staring. Sadie took a calming breath. "Asleep. I saw him sleeping under the bushes. He's okay. He needs his rest."

Her father laughed. "Does he have a job I'm not aware of? Something strenuous like furniture moving?"

"You are so funny, Dad," said Sadie. "How did your writing go? Mom, how was class? Wasn't it gorgeous out today? Except for the mosquitoes. They aren't gorgeous. They're, um, itchy."

Her mother got up to refill her water glass, feeling Sadie's forehead as she passed. "My class was fine, thank you. We did the downwardest-facing dog we'd ever done."

Sadie's father leaned back in his chair and stroked his short beard. "And my day was amazing. Early on, as you may recall, I couldn't do anything right. But later everything changed. I hardly know how to describe it. It's like I found my voice again. I wrote four new pages and revised another ten."

Hmmm, maybe the hokey-pokey spell *did* work after all. Just not for the right person.

Her mother stood. "Well, if you guys clean up, I think I'll go hunt for Wilson. Virginia will make a bath mat out of him if she finds him in there again."

Sadie shot to her feet. "I'll look for him. I know just where he is."

"Well, I hope you do," said her father. "We wouldn't want him staying out all night and being late for work."

The sun hung low in the sky as Sadie made her way across the lawn. Soon the grass and bushes would be engulfed by dark. She thought of the birds settling into their nests. Tucking their heads beneath their wings. Closing their eyes. Did birds dream? And if they did, what about? People dreamed about flying. Did birds dream about going shopping or driving a car or eating beetles with a knife and fork?

She crept up to the playhouse and peeked in the window. There she was. Ms. M. Her Ms. M. Asleep on the ducky blanket, Wilson lying doughnut-shaped at her feet.

"Psst! Wilson!" she whispered. The cat raised his head.

"I'm awake, Sadie." Ms. M rolled over to face her. "Come in."

"I'd better not. My parents . . ."

"Grown-ups. I understand."

"I just came to get Wilson. Mom wants him inside. But maybe he can sleep with you tomorrow night. You'll still be here, won't you?"

"Of course." Ms. M's eyes stood out like gems in the gathering dusk.

"We can start looking for Ethel again first thing in the morning."

"I like that plan." The witch gently lifted the floppy cat and passed him through the playhouse window into Sadie's arms.

"Sweet dreams, my dears."

"Sweet dreams, Ms. M."

The sound of her parents laughing together and the clink of dishes being loaded into the dishwasher floated through the open kitchen window. As Sadie crossed the patio, cradling Wilson, she wondered how early she could go to bed without her mother feeling her forehead again. Just this morning she had nothing to look forward to. Now tomorrow couldn't come fast enough.

Chapter 9
Columba livia

Sadie's mother left right after breakfast to teach an eight o'clock class. Her father had already shut himself in the study with a Cranberry Creativity smoothie to try to, as he put it, "recreate the magic of yesterday."

Sadie set her half-full cereal bowl in the sink and rushed outside.

"Ms. M? Ms. M?"

No matter how loudly she knocked, Ms. M didn't answer. Either the witch was a heavy sleeper or— Sadie opened the playhouse door and peered in.

She could almost hear Maya: *vanished, evaporated, dematerialized*. But they all meant the same thing.

Gone.

Poof.

"Up here!"

On a medium-high branch of the maple tree, a crow with an intelligent expression shook its feathers and nodded in her direction.

"Ms. M! Not you, too!"

"No, dear. Up here. On top of the garage."

Now Sadie saw her. Scooting down the

side of the roof that faced Sadie's mother's meditation garden, the witch waved merrily with one hand and clutched a red-handled broom with the other.

A broom! Today promised to be even more exciting than Sadie had thought.

"Can you give me a turn?" she called, picturing herself doing loop-de-loops over her house, over the neighborhood, over the whole city. Maybe even all the way to Moose Butt Lake.

"That's lovely of you to volunteer, but I'm more or less finished."

Sometimes Ms. M made no sense. "Finished flying?"

"Flying?" The witch sounded genuinely puzzled.

"On your broom. I'd like a turn on your broom, please. I promise I'll be careful."

Ms. M reached the bottom of the roof slope. She sat on the edge, her skinny legs dangling. "Sorry to disappoint you, dear, but I just brought this old broom up with me in case the gutters needed cleaning. And I'm glad I did. I'm surprised your parents don't know that keeping gutters and downspouts in good condition requires regular maintenance. Now, would you mind holding the ladder steady while I climb down?"

The witch indicated with the broom the spot where, indeed, a ladder leaned against the garage wall, partly concealed by the rhododendron bush.

"How about if I come up?" It wasn't exactly magical, but a rooftop adventure sounded okay, too. Though perhaps she should run back inside first to trade her flip-flops for shoes with better grip.

"Don't you dare. My spells for mending broken hearts and broken promises are almost always reliable, but my spell for mending broken arms takes six weeks to six months to work."

A sweet, dusty scent tickled Sadie's nose. A comforting smell, growing stronger as Ms. M wobbled down the rungs toward her.

When the soles of Ms. M's pointy shoes clanked onto the last rung, Sadie stepped back. "Thank you," the witch said, hopping to the ground. She detached a clump of brown leafy muck from the broom's bristles and flung it onto the grass. "Your parents really should consider hiring someone."

"Were you looking for Ethel?"

"Always. Though when I climbed up, I did

observe a pair of *Columba livia.*" Ms. M smiled and gazed upward. "Remarkable specimens. But then, all of them are." She returned her focus to Sadie. "'*Columba livia*' means 'dove the color of lead' in Latin. Such regal birds."

Fancy doves! Just Sadie's luck to have missed them. "Are they still there?" she asked. "Can I borrow your binoculars?"

"No need. I'll call them down. So you can meet in person."

Ms. M fluttered her lips. "ppbbbBBBRRR!" She puffed out her stomach and quickly sucked it back in. She did it again. "Some warm-up exercises," she explained. "To engage my diaphragm."

Dove calls must be difficult. Sadie didn't know if she'd ever heard a dove before. When she tried to remember, all she could think of were pictures in books. Pictures of snow-white doves carrying olive branches in their beaks or popping out of magicians' hats.

After a few jaw and neck stretches, during which Ms. M's hat tipped precariously but somehow did not fall off, she said, "Okay. Now I'm ready."

Sadie waited. Any moment now. . . .

"Bob! Lois!"

Hwhapwhapwhapwhap.

With a flurry of wings, two gray birds landed on the driveway.

Chapter 10
Rare Birds

"Pigeons."

Ms. M beamed. "Sadie, for a beginner your identification skills are really coming along."

The pigeons strutted back and forth in a tight zigzag pattern, one behind the other as if playing a game of follow-the-leader.

"Not to be rude," Sadie said tentatively.

"But everyone can identify pigeons. Pigeons are EVERYWHERE." She spread her arms wide, startling the bird in front—Bob? Lois?—into strutting faster and leading his— her?—companion closer to Ms. M.

"You'd think so, wouldn't you?" the witch mused, bending down. From the front pocket of her dress she retrieved a small handful of sunflower seeds and scattered them on the pavement. "But Bob and Lois have to fly all the way over to the awning of the Thai restaurant on Hawthorn Street to visit their nearest daughter." She looked at the birds. "Did you say her name was Karen?" It was hard to tell whether Bob and Lois nodded or simply dipped their heads to reach their snack.

"Okay," Sadie said. "Do they really have names? Or are you making that up?"

"Pigeons have lived among us for more than ten thousand years. They've picked up many of our habits and customs. And, unfortunately, our germs." She nodded toward the bird on her right. "Lois accepted Cheerios from a boy with a runny nose." Then, to Lois, "Did the echinacea help?"

Lois made a noise deep in her chest—a cough? A coo? Again, it was hard to tell. At least Sadie now knew which bird was which. The more she looked, the more differences she noticed. Dark spots dappled Lois's light gray wings, whereas Bob's wings had no pattern other than the two wide dark stripes at the bottom. Lois's wings had stripes, too, but, unlike Bob's, they were scalloped at the edges, like lace around a valentine heart. Standing sideways facing each other, the birds resembled giant, slightly mismatched salt and pepper shakers.

"I need to get something from inside the playhouse," Ms. M said, straightening. "I'll be right back."

Once Ms. M left, Sadie looked at Bob and Lois. Bob and Lois looked at Sadie.

"I had a cold, too," Sadie said to break the silence. "Last week. But I'm pretty much over it."

Bob lifted a foot to scratch his neck. Lois wandered toward the petunias.

What were Jess and Maya doing right now?

Cartwheeling across the beach? Diving off the dock? Eating sundaes bigger than their heads?

What was Sadie doing right now?

Making small talk with pigeons. And boring them to death.

"Found it!" the witch said as she reemerged with a tattered notebook.

Sadie stared. Anything could be in there. Spells. Hexes. Enchantments. Or, knowing Ms. M, recipes and bowling scores.

"It's my life list." Ms. M turned to a middle page dense with scribbled text. "Almost all the birds I've seen since I started recording, and that goes back a long time."

"You keep a list? Of birds?"

"It's what birders do." She produced a pen. Out of, it seemed, thin air.

"You didn't have it with you at the park yesterday."

"Already you have the keen eye of a veteran birder." The witch gave her a look of such obvious appreciation that Sadie blushed and ducked her head. "You're right," Ms. M acknowledged. "Sometimes I like to watch and enjoy without the bother of writing everything down. Also, yesterday we were looking for one specific bird. If we'd found Ethel I wouldn't have taken notes, I would have given her a big hug. But I certainly want to record our meeting with Bob and Lois."

At the sound of their names the birds stood up taller, it seemed.

"Different birders organize their lists differently." Ms. M tapped the page with the pen. "As you can see, I have an entire section devoted to *Columba livia*. They're quite extraordinary."

More like ordinary-ordinary, Sadie couldn't help thinking.

Ms. M studied Sadie's face. "You seem skeptical."

"It's just that . . ." She leaned in close to the witch's ear, hoping Bob and Lois wouldn't overhear. She whispered, "It's just, like I said before, pigeons are everywhere."

"Common, yes," said Ms. M at normal volume. "But nonetheless rare. Let me put it to you this way. How many nine-year-old girls are there in the world? Millions? Billions?"

"A lot," Sadie agreed.

"And how many witches?"

Sadie shrugged.

"I believe there were five hundred and seventy-three of us who attended the international conference in Brussels last September," said Ms. M. "Which was an

impressive turnout, given the registration fee." She continued, "Now, out of the million-billion-quadrillions of nine-year-old girls in the world, how many of them are you?"

Was this a trick question? "One?" Sadie ventured.

"And out of the smaller but still sizeable number of witches, how many of them are me?"

Sadie considered Ms. M's droopy hat.

Her dusty dress.

Her crooked, snaggletoothed smile.

"One," she said.

"All right then." Ms. M tapped the page with greater insistence. "Time to get down to business."

She wrote the date on a blank line. "We'll add Bob and Lois here. Beneath Dorothy.

Dorothy was lovely. I met her and her brother Toto at an outdoor film festival in Poughkeepsie. Their mother was a great fan of the classics."

Sadie could see that the life list didn't go straight up and down, like a grocery list, but was spread across the page in columns. Next to the date in the first column, Ms. M wrote Bob and Lois's names. "What about the sighting conditions?" she asked. "Stormy? Dense fog? Bitterly cold? Cyclonic?"

"Um, nice?" Sadie suggested.

"We'll say 'very nice.' To reflect the mood of the day. Now, location. You wouldn't happen to know the latitude and longitude of your backyard, would you?"

"Not really."

"We'll just put 'North America, Sadie's backyard.' Last is vocalization, though that can be hard to summarize for *Columba livia*. They are such lively conversationalists."

Ms. M appeared to be concentrating hard. At her feet Bob burbled and cooed. He sounded like a cross between a purring cat and a tiny, whistling freight train.

"Of course, Bob, thank you for reminding me." In the last rectangle of space on the line Ms. M carefully printed "Home."

"What does that mean?" Sadie asked. Was Ms. M thinking of going home after all?

"When we were up on the roof, Bob and Lois told me how much they love where they live. I told them that I wished Ethel had turned into a pigeon instead of a yellow warbler, because then I never would have lost her. Pigeons are home-oriented. They leave, but they always come back."

Hwhapwhapwhap!

Sadie jumped backward in surprise as Lois launched herself into the air, landed on the curve of Ms. M's shoulder, and nuzzled her with her beak.

"Yes, you are absolutely right," said the witch, smiling faintly and patting Lois on the head. "Ethel is who she is. I can't change that."

"What if we went to the park?" said Sadie. "We could try the picnic table by the fountain. I bet we'd have better luck."

"Of course, dear. Would you mind fetching the binoculars? They're in my bag. Put this away for me while you're at it." Ms. M held out the life list. "That's enough note-taking for one day."

Hwhapwhapwhapwhapwhap!

Bob and Lois flung themselves upward, rose over the garage, and kept going. In no time at all they turned from big dots to small dots to smaller dots, finally disappearing altogether.

Poof.

"Wow, pigeons are fast," Sadie said, staring at the spot in the sky where they had just been.

"Champion flyers," Ms. M agreed.

"I hope I see them again."

"Oh, you will," Ms. M said gaily. "They're on their way to the park. They're meeting Karen there for lunch."

Chapter 11
For Sale

Once again they saw a lot of birds.

Once again they heard a lot of birds.

Once again not one of those birds was Ethel.

"I never knew watching and listening could be so tiring," Sadie said. She and Ms. M both wobbled a bit as they left the park, taking the winding path by the tennis courts. "It's a good kind of tired," she added.

"Exhausting and exhilarating at the same time," Ms. M agreed. "Like traveling."

As they ambled along, Sadie thought about how the park really was like another country to her now, full of many languages and exotic inhabitants. In a way, she didn't even mind that they hadn't found Ethel. She and Ms. M could go "traveling" again tomorrow, and maybe the next day and the day after that.

When they reached the backyard, Sadie said, "I wish I could invite you to come inside—"

The witch interrupted. "I know, dear. It's all right. I enjoy my own company."

"I'll be out later to say good night."

"I look forward to it."

Sadie watched Ms. M until she was safely at the playhouse. The witch paused and tipped her pointy hat. Sadie giggled and slipped into the kitchen.

"Is that you, Sadie?" her mother called from upstairs. "Dad ran to the store. I'll be down in a minute."

Sadie sat at the table, munching a granola bar and thinking more about Ethel. What would they do if they did find her? Would Ms. M know the right spell to change her back? She tried to imagine two witches living in the playhouse. Wait until Jess and Maya saw that!

Then she tried to picture herself with Jess, Maya, Ms. M, and Ethel. They'd all be together, doing . . . what? Bird-watching? Sweeping out the gutters? Making soup?

Her father entered the kitchen through the back door, clutching a bag from Paper Warehouse. He hung his keys on the orange hook on the wall and smiled at her. "Tough day at the slide and the merry-go-round, sleepyhead?"

Just then her mother thumped in with a big cardboard box. "So much junk in the attic!" She dropped the box onto the table across from Sadie. "I wish we could get rid of it all, but we'll start here and see what they have room for."

"Your labels, madam," her father said

gallantly, handing over the bag.

"What's going on?" Sadie asked. She got up to pour herself a glass of chocolate milk.

"The Kepplers are having a yard sale tomorrow, and they said we could add a few things. You don't want these anymore, do you?"

Sadie peered down at the dolls with soiled faces, the unopened paint-by-number kit, the squashed board games that she and her parents used to play for hours. The game Sorry! just looked, well, sorry. And the patient in Operation had never fully regained consciousness, not since Mom had accidentally vacuumed up his Funny Bone.

She grabbed Tina Tag-Along and pulled the string on her back, but instead of "Me, too!" Tina now said "Mrggfft."

"Good-bye, Tina," she said, replacing the doll gently in the box.

"All the toy money comes back to you," Dad informed her.

"Really? Cool!" She might earn enough for a field guide if Ms. M didn't find hers.

"What do you think for Chutes and Ladders?" said her mother, pen poised over a sticky label. "Two bucks?"

"Sure."

"The playhouse is a little worse for wear, but it should bring at least twenty dollars."

What? The chocolate milk turned to sludge in Sadie's throat. She sputtered. "We can't sell the playhouse!"

"Why not?" said her father. "You never play in it."

"Yes I do. I did today."

"Remember what the Buddha said." Her mother slapped a sticker onto Diva Dinah's now only somewhat-sequined gown. "Suffering comes from attachment."

Sadie rolled her eyes. "I'm not attached to it. I play in it."

"Look," said her mother firmly. "I am suffering. My back suffers every time I have to move that thing to mow. My eyes suffer when they see the big yellow spot where it's killed all the grass."

Sadie's father went to put his arm around her, but she ducked out of reach. "Some things you can hold on to, honey. Others you have to let go."

"Let go," meaning *lose*? The way Ms. M had lost Ethel and Onyx? And now Sadie would lose . . .

"No!"

"Yes," said her mother in her end-of-discussion tone. "Say good-bye to your playhouse and wish it well. Tomorrow it's moving on."

Chapter 12

Snow Globes and Unicorn Horns

Sadie hurried to the playhouse with the news. The bad news. News so bad, it felt like she was carrying something heavy. Something she couldn't wait to put down.

Without knocking, she burst through the door.

The witch didn't even turn around. Didn't stop taking things out of her apparently bottomless black bag and lining them up on the ground. She was humming to herself. The soft "*m, m, m*"s mingled with an aroma of— what, exactly? Spices, yes, but not cooking spices. Spices from somewhere with a long, mysterious name. Somewhere hot winds blew and animals with bells around their ankles rose and shook themselves free of sleep.

Sadie took a deep breath. Her news—that awful burden—seemed lighter. But still not good.

"There's going to be a yard sale," she began.

Ms. M turned and smiled. "I know. That's why I'm doing a little housecleaning."

"But—"

"First things first, dear. Do you have any of those stickers people use for yard sales? I'd like to price these items."

"But what about—"

"At least three dollars for this." Ms. M held up a stubby yellow pencil.

"It's only an inch long."

"True, but it's a pencil from Pennsylvania. Hear the alliteration? That adds to the value."

Next Ms. M handed her a cloudy snow globe. "From the Sahara. One of a kind."

"It's empty!"

"Sadie, I'm surprised that a clever girl like

you has forgotten that it doesn't snow in the desert." The witch took back the globe. Breathed on it. Polished it with her sleeve. "Ten dollars, don't you think?"

"No, and anyway, what I came to tell you is—"

"What about this?" Ms. M showed Sadie a faded blue T-shirt with writing on it. A lot of writing.

Sadie strained to read the small print. "What does it say?"

Ms. M recited, "I Survived the Two Wicked Stepsisters Zip Line at Prince Charming's

Slip-er-Slide Water Park and Nevertheless All I Got Was This Lousy T-Shirt, Which Isn't Even 100% Cotton and Gives Me Hives." She held the shirt out at arm's length. Tilted her head. Nodded. "Fifteen dollars," she declared, placing it in the growing pile.

"Please, Ms. M, I really need—"

"Now, this is the very top of my collection." With a swordsman's flourish, she withdrew a long, thin object from the bag. "A unicorn horn. So many memories! And not all that long ago. Just last Halloween, in fact. Ethel and I went to a neighborhood party. Two other unicorns there, but I was the snazziest." She extended the horn toward Sadie. "You can hold it, but gently, please. It's fragile."

"It's tinfoil wrapped around a stick. With elastic—"

"Oh dear, yes. It's out of context. Let me put it on." Ms. M maneuvered the stick over her hat onto her forehead and secured the elastic strap beneath her chin.

Amazing. She didn't look like a unicorn, but she did look, well, interesting.

"It's very nice, but listen. My parents want to sell the—"

"Such a wonderful party," Ms. M interrupted dreamily, galloping a few steps forward and a few steps back. "We danced the night away. And Ethel won a prize! Most Authentic Costume. Which was a miracle. She's so scattered! First she wanted to go as a salad, but couldn't decide between ranch

and French. Then it was a woolly mammoth, but that itched and was tight under the arms. Finally she just went as herself."

"As a witch?"

"No, as her authentic self. The real Ethel. There's nothing as attractive as someone being her true, true self. Especially when she's doing the mambo with a unicorn."

Sadie couldn't help but smile even as she—finally!—announced, "Mom and Dad want to sell the playhouse."

"Yes, I suppose we should put all our energies there." The witch took off the unicorn horn. She returned it to the bag, followed by the T-shirt and the snow globe. "I can't part with any of these things, anyway. They are positively vibrating with memories."

Chapter 13
Plan B

The next morning Sadie and Ms. M stood out by the compost bin, beside the bubbling cauldron. The witch was dressed in another one of Sadie's old outfits, complete with shoes—Sadie's last-year soccer cleats.

"Reminds me of my college days on the

Dragonville Stompers," said Ms. M, taking an enthusiastic kick at the air.

"You played soccer?"

"Stomp ball," said the witch. She brought her foot down on a large white mushroom cap to demonstrate.

"It's strange," said Sadie, "how Dad and Mr. Keppler don't seem to notice you."

"They notice me. They just don't see me. Or, rather, they see what they want to see. They see you with your little friend."

"You don't look like any of my other friends. You look like a witch in my clothes and a Milwaukee Brewers baseball cap."

"Not to them."

"Okay, my friend, they're about to carry away the playhouse." Sadie pointed to the cauldron. "So I hope that hex you're working on will stop them."

The witch took a brimming spoonful, slurped, smiled, and nodded. "Perfect."

Sadie's father and Mr. Keppler lifted the playhouse and started slowly across the yard. "It isn't working!" Sadie wailed. "They're almost to the street!"

"This isn't a hex, Sadie. It's oatmeal. Source of iron, phosphorous, and zinc. Have a taste." Ms. M held out the spoon, but Sadie pushed it away.

"Don't you understand? They're going to sell your house. We have to do something."

"Well, I do have a nice little hex that will wrinkle all their clothes."

"Be serious."

"I could turn them into elephant seals."

"Not that serious."

"You're right. You do not want to live with an elephant seal. They take up all the room in the Jacuzzi. Let me think for a moment."

Silently Ms. M stirred and stirred. Sadie fidgeted so hard that she woke up Wilson, who glared at her and moved under a fern.

"I know," Ms. M said after a while. "I'll make it rain. No one likes to drip and shop."

Sadie exhaled in relief. "That sounds great.

And you're sure you can do it?"

The witch reached into a cluster of plants, waved away a spider, took a pinch of its web, and dropped it into the cauldron. Then she added a few more things from her deep black bag.

"I thought that was oatmeal," said Sadie.

"It is. But now in addition to being high in fiber it also summons storms' fury."

Sadie surveyed the sky. "No fury so far."

"Let's try again," said Ms. M. She reached for Sadie's hand. "Repeat after me: water clear and water bright, wash away this sale tonight."

"It's not night, it's nine a.m."

"So it is. Water clear, a gentle spray, wash away this sale today."

"A gentle spray isn't going to wash away anything."

"No, but such a lovely use of imagery. When I took Omens & Augury, everybody envied my facility with language."

Overhead was still blue, blue, and more blue. The only clouds were wispy and white and decidedly nonthreatening. No sudden gust of wind. No smell of moisture in the air.

Nothing.

It was time for Plan B. Plan S, actually. Plan Sadie.

"Come with me, Ms. M. I've got a better idea."

Chapter 14
Toxic Fumes

In the Kepplers' driveway, they joined the crowd milling among the stacks of books and plates, the treadmill and the microwave, the clothes hanging on racks or spread out on the ground in neat piles.

"Only three dollars," said Ms. M, lifting the lid on a Crock-Pot. "I could cook a whole gremlin in here!"

"We'll shop later," whispered Sadie. "Look." She pointed to a little girl tugging her mother over to the playhouse, which stood off to the side between a cluster of ski boots and a floor lamp shaped like a palm tree.

The witch began chanting rapidly, "Watercleanandwaterbright . . ."

"Too late for that," said Sadie. "Wait here."

She slipped around behind the playhouse and slithered in through the back window. When the little girl and her mother got close enough, Sadie flung herself through the front door, one hand clutching her throat.

"Toxic fumes," she gasped, and collapsed in the grass.

The witch chimed in, "I used to be a

happy, healthy eight-year-old. I had tea in that playhouse yesterday, and now look!"

She took off her baseball cap to reveal gray, matted hair.

Ms. M and Sadie high-fived as the mother hurried her daughter away.

Next the witch sidled up to a man tapping his knuckles on the playhouse roof, as if he was checking a watermelon for ripeness. "My great-aunt Matilda died in there," she told him. "But don't worry. It wasn't contagious."

"Is that so?" said the man, looking amused. "What was your aunt doing in a children's playhouse?"

"Her doctors blamed delirium. From the fever brought on by the infected bile," said the witch, hacking loudly into her cupped hands. "Oh, my." She let the man see the yellowy-green slime streaking her palm. "Would you mind feeling my forehead?"

The man bought a beanbag chair instead.

Ms. M grinned and wiped her hand on her sweatpants. "Turns out I had a smidge of llama drool left after all."

"This is fun!" said Sadie. She approached a mom who was trying to stuff a whining toddler back into his stroller.

"You should buy him that playhouse. It's a bargain, considering how much my parents paid the exterminator." Sadie scratched at her arms and chest. "Did you know that bedbugs don't just live on beds?"

"Sadie!" It was Mr. Keppler. He motioned her over to the sale table.

"Cover for me," she told the witch.

Mr. Keppler opened the money box, jam-packed with bills. "Big profits today, young lady, but no bites yet on the playhouse.

Try marking it down to fifteen dollars." He winked. "That should catch us a fish."

Shoving the pen he gave her into her sock, Sadie turned from the sale table in time to see two little boys dressed as superheroes—one Batman, one Spider-Man—dash into the playhouse and then stagger back out holding their capes in front of their noses.

She hurried over to where Ms. M leaned against a tree, fanning herself.

"What happened?" Sadie asked.

"I transmuted some energy to make the playhouse undesirable. A simple combination of nitrogen, methane, carbon dioxide, and hydrogen."

"You what?"

"I farted in the living room."

They laughed together as other yard sale items continued to disappear, but the playhouse remained solidly in place. Eventually the crowd dwindled to two older women haggling over the price of a lopsided dresser.

Ms. M let out a yawn so big that covers on the fifty-cent paperbacks fluttered. She rested her chin on a stack of flowered pillowcases—now three for a dollar—and closed her eyes.

Sadie knew how she felt. After all of their brilliant performances, she didn't think she had the strength left to talk to even one more customer. But it looked like she wouldn't have to. The garage sale was almost over. Across the driveway, Mrs. Keppler started boxing up unsold cups and plates.

Just then a blue station wagon pulled to the curb. A woman and man got out. The man opened the passenger door, and Sadie groaned as she watched him unstrap a baby from a car seat.

Smiling, the young family headed straight toward the playhouse.

Chapter 15

Priceless

"Go get that blanket," instructed the witch. "The one you loaned me. It's in my bag."

"But we can't nap now—"

"Trust me. And hurry."

Sadie sprinted across the street and returned in less than a minute.

"What's this for?"

"To make the playhouse invisible."

"Oh, good, you found the wolfsbane."

Ms. M shook her head. "It's magical enough because it's yours. It has your essence all through it."

With that she tossed the ducky blanket onto the playhouse roof.

"But it doesn't cover it at all!" Sadie said, dizzy with panic.

"All prices negotiable," Mr. Keppler cheerily informed the man and woman as they started up the driveway. "Just make me an offer."

"It's invisible now," said the witch.

"It's not! It's totally not!" The playhouse shimmered behind her stinging tears like a fairy castle in the mist. But it would soon vanish into the back of that station wagon.

Poof.

The young couple was only a few feet away.

"Looks like all the cool toys are gone," Sadie heard the woman say as the family strolled past.

"There are other yard sales," said the man. He bounced the baby against his hip. "Aren't there, kiddo?" The couple turned around and walked hand in hand back toward the street.

"What did I tell you?" said Ms. M.

"They saw it, they just didn't like it."

"No, they didn't like it because they didn't see."

Sadie felt a tap on her shoulder. "Excuse me. Do you know how much they want for this?" A man in a suit gestured to the playhouse. His tie was loose, and he looked tired.

"Fifty dollars," answered Ms. M, arms crossed.

"I'd pay twenty." The man reached into his back pocket for a battered leather wallet.

"Fifty," she insisted. "That's the minimum."

"Well, somebody is living in a yard sale dreamworld."

As he stomped away, Ms. M said to Sadie, "He didn't see it either."

"Are you crazy? He offered twenty dollars for it."

"He didn't see it deeply, dear. He didn't see its real value. Its essence. Its light. It's like the stars. They're out there in the sky every night. Wondrous things. But most people don't even bother to look up. And speaking of up . . ."

While they'd been talking, a patch of dark clouds had moved in and gobbled up the last of the afternoon sun. All the customers still in the driveway—there weren't many—bolted for their cars.

"Better late than never," Ms. M cackled as the first drops fell on her gnarled, outstretched hand.

Chapter 16

The Ornithomancer's Guide

To celebrate, Sadie brought two Freezee Treats out to the backyard.

She gave Ms. M first pick. "Banana or grape?"

"Ah, noble grapes, food of Bacchus, the god of wine and mirth."

"No kidding?" Sadie said, handing her friend the purple one.

"Also, fake banana flavor?" Ms. M made a face. "Bleh."

They watched from behind the rhododendron bush as her father and Mr. Keppler returned the playhouse to its proper place. "This thing is heavier than it was this morning," they heard her father complain. "It's cursed!"

Ms. M poked her head out. "Well, technically—" Sadie clamped a hand over her mouth and pulled her back into hiding.

When it was safe to come out, they spread the ducky blanket over the rain-dampened grass and sat on it together, slurping happily. Wilson entertained them by crouching, wriggling his behind, and springing at flies.

"Onyx was a first-rate fly catcher," the witch said, and she sucked the last drip of juice from the Freezee Treat wrapper.

Sadie found herself thinking about how she would feel if Wilson went missing, if she had only a cat-shaped emptiness instead of his warm, furry self.

"I was lonely," she blurted, "until you came along."

"Me, too," said Ms. M.

From high in the maple tree, a robin tried four or five notes four or five different ways.

They both reached for their binoculars and scanned the yard. At one point their eyes met through their lenses, and they giggled.

Ms. M lowered her binoculars and looked directly at Sadie. "I like to think that Onyx has found a nice new home."

"But you don't know that for sure."

"But I don't *not* know it. Is my tongue purple?"

"Weirdly enough, it's green."

"Excellent. A spell that works."

Sadie laughed. "What about my tongue?" She opened wide.

"The exact shade of Ethel's belly. Which reminds me . . ."

She popped into the playhouse and popped back out waving a book, which she tossed onto Sadie's lap. "I found my field guide!"

"*The Ornithomancer's Guide to the Upper Midwest.*" Sadie read the title aloud slowly.

"The deluxe edition includes hippogriffs, but they're mainly in the Southeast."

Sadie turned the pages carefully, so as not to smudge them with her sticky fingers. Grackles and grebes. Shrikes and swallows.

The great blue heron and the common loon. So many amazing birds!

And there, on page 198, the yellow warbler. The bird in the photo was a male, the guide said, because of the reddish streaks on his otherwise lemon-colored breast. He gazed sideways at the camera with a round, black, inquisitive eye.

"You know what I was thinking?" Sadie didn't wait for an answer. "That it'd really be fun to be a different kind of bird-watcher and not watch all the birds sometimes but just one bird all the time. And follow him wherever he went and watch him there."

"You're a very interesting young woman," said Ms. M.

Embarrassed, Sadie pretended to be

studying the habitat map for the ring-necked pheasant. "Wait until you meet Jess and Maya. They're a lot more interesting than I am."

Ms. M laughed so loudly that the mourning doves perched on the telephone wire stopped crying. She placed her old, rough hand on Sadie's young, smooth one. "Such a generous thing to say. And so not true."

"When you were my age," Sadie asked softly, closing the field guide, "did you know you wanted to be a witch?"

"I just wanted to be like my mother. We lived in the forest. My father was a botanist, and he traveled a lot. My mother taught me most of what I needed to know. The forest taught me the rest." Suddenly Ms. M stared hard at the lilacs. "Look there."

A flash of yellow!

Eventually the witch shook her head. "Eastern meadowlark. They build their nests on the ground, of all things."

"What if we never find Ethel?" asked Sadie.

Ms. M polished one lens of her binoculars with the corner of her smock. Then she polished the other lens. "Things change," she said after a while. "That's what living in the forest taught me. Trees die and new ones grow. Wolves I could recognize in the fall didn't come back in the spring. And what if Ethel likes being a bird? Probably she has a mate and children by now. It's what birds do."

"So are you going to give up looking for her?"

"No. I will always look. I like looking.

Maybe it will lead me to Ethel, and maybe it won't, but either way, I have wonderful memories." She laid the binoculars in her lap. "Ethel and I were close for a long time. And now I have a new friend and a new place to live."

"My parents still want to sell the playhouse," Sadie warned.

Once again the robin in the maple tree sang out. *Cheery-o, churlee, cheery-up!*

"An intriguing vocalization," Ms. M said. "Certainly territorial."

The witch pursed her lips and replied to the robin. Sadie wasn't exactly sure what the witch's lilting melody meant, but she figured it was something along the lines of, *Don't worry, I won't take your nest. I have my own.*

Chapter 17

Sparks!

"Ready for Taco Night?" Sadie asked Wilson, who was sprawled out next to her on the window seat. "I wish Onyx was here. Ms. M says refried beans are his favorite."

She put down *Birds of Lore and Legend*. It was a good book, but she couldn't concentrate, not with the yummy smell of onions and chili powder wafting over from the playhouse.

In the backyard, a jittery wren landed on the feeder Sadie had bought that morning at the garden supply store with some of her yard sale money. She liked knowing that it was a wren and not a sparrow or a nuthatch. She liked watching birds closely and noticing their differences. They didn't all look the same, and they didn't all act the same, either. Some were shy. Some were bold. Some were show-offs. Some were copycats.

She petted Wilson. "If you could read, you'd love *Birds of Lore and Legend*. It would be like a menu to you and Onyx."

Wilson's eyes closed completely. He

arched his back more deeply under her hand.

"Onyx," Sadie said, her gaze following the ribbon of smoke that meant dinner was almost ready. "Ms. M really misses you. Please come back. Please."

Her hand began to tingle as if it were falling asleep. Then, suddenly, sparks! Crackling between her fingertips and Wilson's fur. Instantly awake, the cat shot out through the open window. He hated static electricity. Which was all that was, wasn't it?

Except that when Wilson reached the hydrangea at the edge of the garden, he stopped. Crouched. Flattened his ears.

The hydrangea swayed. Swayed more. A small black nose parted the thick stems and quickly retreated.

The nose might belong to any neighborhood cat. It might belong to a rabbit or to a raccoon. Or it might . . .

Sadie raced through the kitchen, clattered out the back door, and sped to the playhouse.

She knocked, and there was Ms. M, a brightly colored Mexican serape draped over her shoulders and spilling down the front of her black dress.

"There's something in the bushes," Sadie said, panting. "It might be Onyx."

"Wonderful! Wait just a moment." She returned with her wooden spoon coated in refried beans.

Sadie tossed the hissing Wilson back indoors, and together she and Ms. M advanced toward the hydrangea, Ms. M wielding the crusty spoon like a magic wand. Together they kneeled in the grass.

"See anything?" Ms. M whispered.

"Just leaves. And dirt." Her hopes sank as she examined the shadows beneath the

branches. Maybe she'd imagined the nose after all.

But then one of the shadows began to move.

The shadow sprouted sleek black fur and whiskers.

The shadow blinked its golden eyes.

The shadow stuck out its small pink tongue and lapped at the witch's spoon.

"Hello, my dear boy." Ms. M waited until he was finished, handed Sadie the spoon, and gathered Onyx into her arms. She kissed his small black nose. She kissed it again.

Sadie reached to pet Onyx. The witch intercepted her hand. Held it tight. "Thank you, Sadie. You found my cat for me."

"I didn't do anything. He just came back."

"Really?" Ms. M pressed her fingertips against Sadie's. The connection between them was warm. Electric. "If I opened my field guide, would you be listed as solitary, drab, shy, and retiring? I don't think so."

Chapter 18
Adios

"Let's get into the spirit of things!" From her bag, the witch pulled a sombrero with gold tassels and plunked it onto Sadie's head. "A perfect fit."

Next she grabbed her broomstick, spun around twice, and lightly tapped the goldfish-shaped piñata hanging in the corner. "For after supper," she said, teetering a bit before regaining

her balance. "If the cats are interested."

"Onyx likes candy?" asked Sadie.

"Oh, yes. Especially M&Ms. Which in this case means Mackerel and Mahi-Mahi. But for us, right now, some savory *carne asada*."

"It looks really good."

"It *is* really good! Hold out your bowl."

Sadie and Ms. M sat against the sturdy walls and ate. After a few cautious sniffs and growls, Wilson and Onyx had settled down and were—miracle of miracles—side by side, sharing a small red saucer of beans. Sadie wished she had a camera. She could show the picture to Jess and Maya and say, "Sorry you

missed our fiesta. It was so much fun." Maybe she could convince Ms. M to leave the chili pepper lights wrapped around the rim of the cauldron for one more day so Jess and Maya could see them.

Tomorrow. Her friends would be home tomorrow. How had four whole days gone by?

Time was such a shifty thing. Like the great horned owl at the park yesterday. When Sadie had turned away to watch a gaggle of Canada geese totter across the bike path and then almost immediately turned back, the owl was gone. As if it had never been there.

"More guacamole?" Ms. M passed her the

bowl. "I got the recipe from a *bruja* who lives just outside Puerto Vallarta. Carmelita will be so excited to see Onyx again! We used to spend every winter with her, but it's been a while."

Wilson jumped up onto a black suitcase and began cleaning himself. A suitcase? That meant . . . Sadie dropped her taco. "You're leaving."

Ms. M nodded. "I dreamed Ethel was in Mexico. And even if she's not, *El Gato Grande* deserves a little fun in the sun after all he's been through, don't you agree?"

"But you can't!"

"Why not?"

"Well, because . . . I mean . . . you just can't."

"You'll be fine. I'll write to you."

"That's what Jess and Maya said." Sadie blinked back tears. The walls tilted and spun as if the playhouse were a carnival ride.

"I'm sure their postcards are in the mail." Ms. M squeezed Sadie's hand. Then she reached down beside her for the field guide. "Hold on to this for me while I'm gone. You watch for Ethel here. I'll watch for her there.

I have a good feeling she'll turn up."

The weight of the book in Sadie's lap felt solid. Steady. "So you're really going."

"I really am. But that doesn't mean I won't be back." The witch smiled. She had a green speck of jalapeño stuck between her front teeth. "Keep an eye on Bob and Lois, will you? If Lois's cough gets worse, you might try letting her perch in the bathroom while you shower. The steam will ease her congestion."

Sadie managed a small grin. "Sure. I'll lend her a sweatshirt and a baseball cap. My parents will think she's my new friend from the park. It worked for you."

Cackling, Ms. M stood up and opened a cat carrier that sat beside the battered roll-on suitcase. Onyx walked right in.

"Can I go with you?" asked Sadie. "Just to the street?"

"You know what would be best? If you would check the cauldron to make sure I turned it off. Fire safety is important. Also, would you mind getting the door for me, please?"

Without thinking, Sadie opened the door. Ms. M staggered through with her belongings and bumped it closed behind her. Sadie stood with Wilson in the playhouse for a second before she cried, "Wait!" and rushed out into the yard.

Deserted. There was the lawn in all its greenness. The sky in all its blueness. The house in its houseness. But no tiny woman. No giant suitcase. No cat carrier.

Poof.

A dark, speckled bird landed on the feeder.

A grackle? Before she could open the field guide, her mother stepped onto the back patio holding the white phone. "Sadie? I just talked to Jess's mom. The girls can't wait to see you tomorrow." She started back inside and stopped. "Honey? Why are you wearing a sombrero?"

Chapter 19
Flock Together

Kestrel

Red-winged blackbird

Cedar waxwing

She'd filled one sheet of notebook paper and part of another, and she was still going.

Ostrich

Emperor penguin

Peacock

(Because birds at the zoo counted, right?)

Sadie was starting her life list. From memory. Of course she couldn't recall all of the details—the dates and sighting conditions and whatnot—so she left those columns blank. It made her list look less than official, but she didn't mind. As Ms. M had said, different birders did things differently.

She was surprised to realize how many species she'd seen. A bunch! More than she'd remembered before she started writing them all down.

When she finished, she turned to a clean page and began listing birds that she really wanted to see.

Birds with goofy names like the bufflehead,

the gadwall, and the northern shoveler.

Birds with beautiful plumage like the snowy egret, the purple gallinule, and the painted bunting.

Birds that gave her the shivers like the black vulture and the common raven and the mute swan.

Birds that sang *potato chip, potato chip* (the American goldfinch) or *how looooong?* (the hooded merganser) or *zoooo-zeeee-zoozoo-zeeee!* (the black-throated green warbler).

In order to find these birds, the field guide said, she'd have to go all over. To weedy fields and brushy deserts and restaurant parking lots. To rocky coasts and wide-open marshland. To the shores of deep lakes.

Jess and Maya had probably paddled

their kayaks right by loons or ruddy ducks and didn't even know it. They'd probably shared the beach with mergansers and herring gulls and maybe even moose birds—Canada jays that use moose as buffet tables, eating fleas and ticks straight off the moose backs. Sadie wanted to tell Jess and Maya about Canada jays. She had a lot she wanted to tell them.

After all, she'd been traveling, too.

Pressing down hard with her pencil, she added one more bird to her wish list—Ethel—just as the doorbell rang.

She opened the door and, poof!

Her friends were there.

"Doesn't it seem like we were gone forever?" Jess asked. The three of them stood in the hallway untangling from a group hug.

Jess wore a pair of red shorts overalls Sadie had never seen before. Maya had on new sandals, and each of her toenails was painted a different color. Still, their arms around her felt the same as always.

"*Namaste*, girls!" her mother, in cobra pose, called out as they passed the living room on their way to Sadie's bedroom.

"That's yoga language for 'nice to see you,'" Sadie said.

"Hope you're thirsty for smoothies," her father called from the kitchen. "My soon-to-be-world-famous Banana Blast-Off with spirulina!"

"The little store by the lake sold smoothies," Jess told Sadie. "But—"

Maya interrupted her. "The blender was right by the bait box."

Jess made a face. "Mango Minnow with Mud. Yuck."

Alone with the door closed, the girls settled themselves on the bed. Jess looked at Maya. Maya looked at Jess. Jess looked away. Finally, Sadie asked, "So you guys had fun?"

A long pause, and then Maya said, "Well, it rained a little."

"A lot," Jess admitted.

"Copiously," Maya said. "The closest we got to swimming was sweating in our bunks."

"We stayed in the cabin mostly, with the heat turned way up," Jess explained. "My grandparents are cold all the time."

"There wasn't even a TV! Just back-gammon." Maya groaned. "You know how many channels backgammon has? One. The Boring Network." She turned to Jess. "Not that BeMaw and BePaw aren't really nice, it's just . . . you know."

Jess fiddled with the lace of her high-top sneaker. "We talked a lot about you and what you were doing and how we kind of wished we were back here with you." Her eyes met Sadie's. "What were you doing?"

Sadie took a deep breath. "It's kind of hard to—"

"Were you bereft?" Maya asked plaintively. "Disconsolate? Crestfallen?"

"What?"

"Did you miss us?" Maya translated.

"Of course!"

"Well then, your souvenirs!" Jess started pulling things from her gray satchel and spreading them out on the bed. "Let's see, a Moose Head Lake pen, Moose Head Lake sunglasses—like we needed those—Moose Head Lake lip gloss that tastes like bark. Don't ask. Moose Head Lake cherry raisin fudge, which I would totally give to your parents if I were you. And this cool feather we found on our nature walk before it started hailing."

Sadie picked up the feather. It was lovely. Small and shapely. A vivid yellow with just a hint of black at the tips. When she twirled it between her fingers, it seemed to throw off light.

Could it be?

"It's kind of gross," Jess apologized.

"I swished it around in a puddle to wash off the germs," Maya said.

"It's not gross," Sadie said quietly. Then louder, "I love it. I'm looking for a bird with feathers exactly this color. I met this lady the day you guys left. She was really into bird-watching."

"What lady?" asked Jess. "A friend of your mom's?"

Sadie bounced to the edge of the bed. "Long story." She stood up. "Want to walk to the park with me? We can look for the bird who lost this feather, and I'll tell you what I did while you were gone."

As soon as their feet hit the sidewalk, Jess pointed toward a bush in the yard next door. "Okay, nature expert," she said, as Jess-like as ever. "What are those?" A flock of tiny birds with gray crested heads and white chests were arranged on different branches like football fans on bleachers.

"I don't know." Sadie reached into her back pocket for the well-worn guide Ms. M had left her. "But I'll find out."

Ms. M's Birding Tips

Go outside! Whether you are in New Zealand or New Jersey, a park or a parking lot, chances are, birds are there.

Although birders are sometimes called "twitchers," try to stay still and quiet. Pretend you're a tree. A blue jay might land on you. Or pretend you're a statue. A pigeon might . . . well, maybe not a statue.

There's more to birding than watching. Don't forget to listen. You might hear a chickadee introducing himself—*chicka dee dee dee*—or a pileated woodpecker drumming on a pine.

Everyone enjoys a snack. Set up a feeder in

your backyard or on your apartment balcony and watch customers flock to the Happy Beak Café.

Speaking of snacks, cats do more than watch. It's best to keep kitty indoors.

Field guides are handy, and not just in fields. Who was that dapper orange fellow with the black wings singing outside the window during math class? A good field guide will tell you—after you finish your quiz, dear.

Find a comfortable backpack or satchel to carry gear such as binoculars, notebooks, pencils, and—if you'll be out walking for a while—water and a sack lunch. Unless you prefer writing your field notes in invisible ink, leave the wolfsbane home.

If you're feeling artistic, try drawing

what you see. Sometimes I'm in a hurry and settle for little hints: that sparrow had a ring around its eye; that one had a notch in its tail. Anybody can draw an eye or a tail!

Birding alone is nice. Birding with a friend can be splendid.

A life list is just that—birds I've seen for as long as I've been birding. My life list is like a diary or a journal. I can look back and remember where I was when I saw my first bird, a house finch. I remember his red head and cheerful song. And when he flew, he bounced like a small plane in rough air.

Are you starting a life list? Good for you! What lucky bird will be first?

Satchel

binoculars

guidebook

BIRDS

H₂O

Something to write with

notebook

Snacks

Have You Seen This Bird?

Female yellow warbler (*Setophaga petechia*). Answers to the name Ethel.

Alert, round black eyes.

Beak like a sharpened pencil.

Dandelion-yellow face and body, darker wings and tail. Male warblers have rust-colored streaks on their chests, but Ethel's chest should be unstreaked, unless she's been eating barbecued spiders!

Last seen in Milwaukee, but could be anywhere in North America or, in colder months, as far south as Mexico or even Peru.

Likely nesting near marshland in willows, alders, lilacs, or raspberry bushes.

May or may not have a mate (the gentleman with the streaks).

Should be wearing her spectacles, but probably not.

REWARD!

If found, please contact:
Sadie or Ms. M
c/o The playhouse
Sadie's backyard
U.S.A.

Magic Books

Brandt, Deanna. *Bird Log Kids: A Kid's Journal to Record Their Birding Experiences*. Cambridge, MA: Adventure Publications, 1998.

Cate, Annette LeBlanc. *Look Up!: Bird-Watching in Your Own Backyard*. Somerville, MA: Candlewick Press, 2013.

Stokes, Donald, and Lillian Stokes. *Stokes Beginner's Guide to Birds: Eastern Region*, and (separate volume), *Stokes Beginner's Guide to Birds: Western Region*. Boston: Little, Brown and Company, 1996.

Thompson, Bill, III. *The Young Birder's Guide to Birds of North America*. Peterson Field Guides. Boston: Houghton Mifflin Harcourt, 2012.

Magic Link

Cornell Lab of Ornithology website, www.allaboutbirds.org

Sadie's Birds